MERRY CHRISTMAS
(English)

God J[...]
(Swedis[...])

Shengdan [...]
(Mandarin Chinese)

Krismasi ya furaha
(Swahili)

Joyeux Noël
(French)

Singdan Ji Fi Lok
(Cantonese Chinese)

Selamat Hari Natal
(Malay)

Maligayang Pasko
(Filipino)

Jwaye Nwel
(Haitian Kreyol)

Feliz Natal
(Portuguese)

FRÖHLICHE WEIHNACHTEN
(German)

NOLLAIG CHRIDHEIL
(Scots Gaelic)

FELIZ NAVIDAD
(Spanish)

MERRY CHRISTMAS
(English)

God Jul
(Swedish)

Shengdan Jie Kuaile
(Mandarin Chinese)

Krismasi ya furaha
(Swahili)

Joyeux Noël
(French)

Singdan Ji Fi Lok
(Cantonese Chinese)

Selamat Hari Natal
(Malay)

Maligayang Pasko
(Filipino)

Jwaye Nwel
(Haitian Kreyol)

Feliz Natal
(Portuguese)

FRÖHLICHE WEIHNACHTEN
(German)

NOLLAIG CHRIDHEIL
(Scots Gaelic)

FELIZ NAVIDAD
(Spanish)

Little Dictionary of Foreign Words Used by Santa

Ajabu – amazing (in Swahili);
Pronounce: A-JA-BU

Fantastisch – fantastic (in German);
Pronounce: FAN-TAS-TISH

Oy vey – oh woe is me, or oh no (in Yiddish);
Pronounce: OI-VAY

Regalos – gifts (in Spanish);
Pronounce: RE-GA-LOS

Santa is . . . all colors
Santa speaks . . . all languages
Santa cares for all children
He cares for you.

Author Bio

Deanne Samuels, PhD, is a writer, researcher and psychologist. She has always loved reading, especially children's books, and would love to share and encourage this love of reading with children. Her favorite thing of all time is traveling, and as a child, would have LOVED to guide Santa's sleigh.

DeanneSamuelsKids.com

The Day Santa Got Sick

written by:
Deanne Samuels

illustrations by:
Oliver Kryzz Sj. Bundoc

On the day before Christmas, Santa got sick. Mrs. Claus made him some hot tea with honey, and he stayed in bed, sniffling and coughing and sneezing all day.

Oy vey, thought Santa, I've never missed a Christmas day.
He pondered and he wondered what to do, in all the
different languages that he knew.
But no solution came to mind.

So, he asked Mrs. Claus.
"Coretta dear, who will drive my sleigh tonight?"

"Rollicking reindeer!" said Rudy, who heard
Santa as he passed by his room.

"Why don't we ask our helpers?" said Mrs. Claus. "*Fantastisch Idea*," said Santa. "Maybe we can find a hard-working elf to do the job."

SANTA FOR A DAY

Mrs. Claus made the big announcement on the toy room floor.
The elves clapped, the reindeer leapt, and the snowman sprang with joy!

What an exciting chance this was going to be for everyone!

Rudy Reindeer was first in line.
"OK, Rudy," said Santa.
"I'm going to ask you just one question."
Rudy nodded his head.
"How would you place all the *regalos* around the Christmas tree?"

Rudy looked at his hooves. Oh no, he didn't have fingers!!! How would he open up the sack? "Sorry Santa," said Rudy in a sad voice. So Rudy and all the other reindeer had to get out of line.

The snowman who guarded the North Pole was the next one to step up to Santa.

"Hello Mr. Snowman."
"Hello Santa," he replied.

"My question for you is. . . how would you deliver the toys to all the hot countries, like Jamaica and Japan, Thailand and Togo, Ethiopia and Ecuador?"

A frozen tear slid down the snowman's face.
"Oh Santa," he wailed.
"I wouldn't be able to do that.
I would melt clean away."
And he too walked out of the line.

Now the only ones left were the elves. Elvin the Elf stepped up to Santa's couch.
"OK, Elvin, how would you know which little girl or boy should get a present?"
Elvin felt his stomach give a strange turn.
Most people didn't know this, but elves couldn't read.
They were extraordinary toy makers, but they hadn't had time to go to school. So all the elves also had to leave the line.
All of them, but one. . .

"I suppose I could lead your sleigh this night,"
said Coretta Claus.

"But what about me?" whispered a little girl elf.
The Clauses looked around and saw Ella Elf, who
they hadn't noticed before.
"I know how to read," Ella said. "I can help with the
lists of girls and boys."

Everyone in the room looked on in anticipation. "Of course you can help with the names!"

Mrs. Claus said excitedly.

"I will carry the sack. And we will both deliver the presents together!"

All of Santa's helpers were so relieved that Christmas wouldn't be cancelled this year.

That night, the snowman and all the elves helped pack up the sleigh.
Ella Elf made sure the list of girls and boys was organized.
And Mrs. Claus hooked up the reindeer for the long night ahead.
Ella's heart was filled with rainbows and butterflies.
She would be going on an amazing adventure with Mrs. Claus, all because she had learned how to read!

Santa waved a hopeful goodbye
as the sleigh took off into the
dark, starry sky.

Mrs. Claus and Ella delivered gifts to Johnny and Dayshawn . . .

. . . to Jomo and Jimiyu . . .

. . . and Daria and Dorota . . .

And finally, the sleigh returned
to the North Pole early,
early the next morning.
Santa's heart burst with pride
when he saw that Ella and Mrs.
Claus had delivered all the gifts.

From that time on, Mrs. Claus and Ella Elf travelled with Santa every Christmas. And forevermore, when you look into the sky on Christmas Eve, you may see Santa, Coretta, and Ella guiding the sleigh into the night.

MERRY CHRISTMAS
(English)

God Jul
(Swedish)

Shengdan Jie Kuaile
(Mandarin Chinese)

Krismasi ya furaha
(Swahili)

Joyeux Noël
(French)

Singdan Ji Fi Lok
(Cantonese Chinese)

Selamat Hari Natal
(Malay)

Maligayang Pasko
(Filipino)

Jwaye Nwel
(Haitian Kreyol)

Feliz Natal
(Portuguese)

FRÖHLICHE WEIHNACHTEN
(German)

NOLLAIG CHRIDHEIL
(Scots Gaelic)

FELIZ NAVIDAD
(Spanish)